# Isabella
## the Air
## Fairy

For Isabelle Hudson, with lots of love

Special thanks to Sue Mongredien

ISBN 978-0-545-60525-0

Previously published as Green Fairies #2: *Isabella the Air Fairy* by Orchard U.K. in 2009.

All rights reserved. Published by Scholastic Inc., 557 Broadway, New York, NY 10012, by arrangement with Rainbow Magic Limited.

12  11  10  9  8  7  6  5  4  3  2  1          14  15  16  17  18  19/0

Printed in the U.S.A.                                          40

This edition first printing, July 2014

# Isabella
## the Air
## Fairy

by Daisy Meadows

SCHOLASTIC INC.

The Earth Fairies must be dreaming
If they think they can escape my scheming.
My goblins are by far the greenest,
And I am definitely the meanest.

Seven fairies out to save the earth?
This very idea fills me with mirth!
I'm sure the world has had enough
Of fairy magic and all that stuff.

So I'm going to steal the fairies' wands
And send them into human lands.
The fairies will think all is lost,
Defeated again — by me, Jack Frost!

# Contents

# Flower Fairy

"Rachel! Kirsty! Hurry up, we need to go!" came a voice from downstairs.

"Coming, Mom!" Kirsty Tate shouted back, putting her hair in a ponytail. "There," she said. "Are you ready, Rachel?"

Rachel Walker, Kirsty's best friend, frowned as she gazed around the bedroom the two girls were sharing. "Almost," she said. "But I don't know where my shoes are. Have you seen them?"

Kirsty shook her head. "Maybe they're in the hall," she suggested.

The girls hurried down to find their parents waiting by the front door. The two families were staying in a cottage together for a week on Rainspell Island. It was a very magical place, as Kirsty and Rachel had discovered the first time they'd been there on vacation. That would always be a summer to remember: Not only had they met each other, but they'd also met some very special fairy friends!

So far, this vacation was proving to be just as exciting. They had only arrived yesterday, but Rachel and Kirsty had already found themselves in another wonderful fairy adventure. This time, they were helping the Earth Fairies with a mission to clean up the world's environmental problems.

Today, the two families were going to Seabury, a town on the mainland. The girls wanted to go to a movie and the grownups were going shopping. Kirsty and Rachel really hoped they'd meet another fairy at some point!

Mr. Walker looked at his watch. "Girls, we have to leave

now if you're going to make it in time for the movie. The ferry to the mainland leaves in ten minutes, and there won't be another one for an hour."

"I can't find my shoes, Dad," Rachel said, hunting all around the hallway closet. "Where could they be?"

Kirsty helped her look, and the girls searched the entire cottage before finally finding the shoes under Rachel's bed.

"At last," said Mr. Tate when they reappeared. "We'll have to drive to the ferry now. There isn't time to walk.

We're cutting it close as it is."

The two families got into the Tates' car and drove off. They arrived at the dock just in time. They pulled the car onto the ferry, and, moments later, the ferry sailed to Seabury. It was a short trip and, before long, the two families were driving into the little town.

It was very busy. A huge traffic jam snaked away from the main street, and the cars crawled along an inch at a time.

"*Ugh,*" Kirsty said, closing her window. "What a disgusting smell!"

"It's the fumes from the traffic," her mom said, wrinkling her nose as an old car went by. A stinky gray smoke puffed out of its muffler.

"I don't know where we're going to park." Mr. Tate sighed and leaned against the steering wheel. "I wish we hadn't brought the car. It would have been much faster to walk."

Rachel bit her lip. It was her fault they were in the car—if only she'd been able to find her shoes more quickly!

6

It took ages for the two families to find a parking lot with open spaces. "At last," Mrs. Tate said when they were finally able to walk into town. "I think you probably missed the start of the movie you wanted, girls, but there should be other movies showing that you could see. There's the theater at the end of the block, look. We'll pick you up in the lobby at four o'clock, OK?"

The girls said good-bye to their parents and headed off, chatting about the movies they could watch instead. Just

before they reached the movie theater, they passed a shop that had large pots of flowers outside. "Look at these gray flowers," Kirsty remarked. "They're very unusual. I've never seen gray flowers before, have you?" Rachel stroked one of the oval petals lightly. To her surprise, the gray came off on her thumb, leaving a streaky white color underneath!

"They're not gray," Rachel said. "It's just the exhaust that's made them *look* gray."

Kirsty gently rubbed another petal. It

had a thin gray film on it, too. "Poor flowers," she said. "Where did all the pollution come from?"

Before Rachel could reply, she saw something glittering at the back of the flower arrangement . . . and then, in a cloud of sparkles, out popped a tiny fairy. It was Isabella the Air Fairy!

# All a Flutter!

Isabella had long brown hair that fell in waves about her shoulders. She wore a wispy purple dress with a bright golden belt and leggings. Kirsty and Rachel were delighted to see her again.

"Hello!" they said in chorus. They had been friends with the fairies for a long time, but it was still exciting to have adventures with a new fairy.

"Hello," Isabella said in a musical voice. "Kirsty and Rachel, right? I met you yesterday."

"That's right," Kirsty said. She and Rachel had visited Fairyland to ask the king and queen for help with improving the environment. There they had met seven fairies, who were all training to earn their magic wands. The fairies were named Nicole, Isabella, Edie, Coral, Lily, Milly, and Carrie. The king and queen had given the fairies a challenge. Their job was to help humans with environmental issues, like pollution and littering. Kirsty and Rachel knew that if this test was successful, the king and queen would let their friends be Earth Fairies forever!

"Hi, Isabella," Rachel said. "Have you found your wand yet? Or can we help you look for it?"

Isabella smiled. "Thank you," she replied. "No, I haven't seen my wand anywhere. And I really need it so I can begin my assignment. It's my job to clean up the air, and the sooner I can start, the better!"

Kirsty nodded, her eyes glancing at the grimy gray petals of the flowers nearby. "This place definitely needs cleaning," she said. "We helped Nicole find her wand yesterday, and we've promised to help all the other Earth Fairies do the same. We can't let Jack Frost get away with his nasty tricks!"

Jack Frost was always up to no good. This time, he'd appeared just as the seven Earth Fairies were about to start their Wand Ceremony. They were each going to receive a special wand to help them do their work. Bertram, a friendly frog footman, had been holding the seven wands, but then Jack Frost's goblins had shown up, snatched the wands, and vanished. "My goblins are the only real green creatures!" Jack Frost had sneered. "And I don't want any silly fairies interfering!" Then he disappeared, too, before anyone could stop him.

The goblins were now hiding in the human world with the wands, and Kirsty and Rachel had promised to track them down.

"I have a rough idea where the goblin with my wand is," Isabella told the girls. "So if you don't mind coming on a little journey with me . . ."

"We'd love to!" Kirsty said at once.

Isabella grinned. "I was hoping you'd say that," she said.

"We have to be back to meet our parents at four o'clock," Rachel reminded her friend.

"That's fine," said Isabella. She took a deep breath. "I think I have enough power to turn you into fairies for the trip." She waved her hands and a shower of shimmering blue fairy dust streamed from her fingertips, swirling all over the girls. As soon as the magic sparkles touched

Kirsty and Rachel, they began to shrink
smaller and smaller.

"We're fairies!" Rachel said excitedly,
as she became the same size as
Isabella. She flapped her
glittery wings, smiling
as she floated off
the ground.
"You certainly
are," Isabella said.
"And now that you're
ready . . . off we go!"
She waved her hands
again. Sparkles swirled from
out of nowhere, lifted the three
of them into the air, and carried them
away.

Kirsty felt tingly. Another fairy
adventure was beginning!

A few moments later, they landed gently. Kirsty and Rachel looked around. They realized that they were on the roof of a building in the town next to Seabury. Below, there was a mass of thick clouds that was impossible to see through. "It's very foggy here," Rachel said.

Isabella looked sad. "That's not fog," she replied. "It's clouds of smog—dirty, smoky air. Doesn't it smell awful?"

Kirsty nodded. "It's horrible," she said.
"It makes my throat hurt."

Just then, a tiny
gray butterfly
fluttered
by. Seeing
the fairies,
she gave
an excited
squeak
and zipped
toward them . . .

but then her antennae drooped. "Oh,"
she said, sounding disappointed. "I
thought you were butterflies like me.
What kind of insect are *you*?"

"We're fairies," Isabella said, and
introduced them all. "Who are

you—and what are you doing all the way up here?"

"I'm Flutter," said the butterfly. "I'm tired of living in the dirty city, so I'm looking for a nice green home and some other butterflies to live with. I haven't had any luck yet."

A tear rolled down her face and splashed onto the roof. "And now I'm lost. Please, will you help me?"

The girls exchanged a glance. They couldn't let Flutter down!

# Goblin Alert

"Of course we'll help," Isabella told the sad butterfly.

"Don't worry," Kirsty said. "We'll find you a home. Come on, let's fly down to the ground. There must be a nice park or a small forest . . . or even somebody's yard that would be good for you."

The three fairies and Flutter set off,

diving down through the air. Flying
through the clouds was hard work. Some
were white and fluffy as usual, but others
were gray and
smelly. Rachel
made the
mistake of
flying
through one
of the dirty
clouds and came
out coughing and
choking. Her eyes watered. "Yuck!" she
sputtered. "That was disgusting!"

They could see the ground beneath
them now, and it was clear that they
were in a much bigger town than
Seabury.

There were a lot of cars on the roads,

but none of them appeared to be moving, because they were all stuck in a huge traffic jam. Flying closer, Kirsty noticed that many cars had only one person inside.

Isabella was sighing unhappily. "If only humans could fly, like fairies!" she said. "No wonder the air is so bad here! If some of those drivers shared their cars, or walked or biked instead of driving everywhere, there would be less traffic on the road, and less pollution in the air."

Kirsty nodded. She was starting to realize that pollution affected everyone and was *caused* by everyone, too. "We have to get our bikes out later this week," she vowed to Rachel. "We could go for a family bike ride around the coves!"

"Good idea," Rachel said. Then her face brightened. "There's some green over there," she said pointing. "Let's fly down to see if we can find a home for Flutter."

Flutter wiggled her antennae, looking happier. "Oh, yes!" she squeaked. "Come on, let's check it out!"

The four of them

fluttered lower and lower. As they got
closer to the patch of green, they realized
that it was a park—perfect! But then
Kirsty frowned. Maybe it wasn't so
perfect after all.

"There's a big cloud over the park,"
she noticed. She wrinkled her nose and
fanned the air in front of her face. "And
it smells really strong—like bad
perfume!"

As they zoomed in closer,
they could see who
had made the
cloud. "It's one
of Jack Frost's
goblins!"
Rachel hissed.
She landed on a
branch of a nearby tree

27

and glared at him. "What is he *doing*?"

The goblin had a can of air freshener in each hand and was spraying them into the air. Around his waist, he wore a belt with even more cans of air freshener attached. He looked like a cowboy, Kirsty thought.

Then her eyes grew wide as she saw what else was strapped to his belt. "Rachel, Isabella, look!" she whispered. "It's Isabella's magic wand!"

"Good eyes!" Isabella cried.

Rachel bit her lip. "I can't believe the goblin is here in the middle of the park, in broad daylight, with a magic wand!" she whispered. "If someone spots him, it'll be a disaster!"

Flutter looked from one fairy to another, not understanding. "Why?" she asked. "Who is this person anyway?" She coughed. "And why does he keep spraying that horrible stuff all around? It smells awful!"

"He's a goblin. If humans find out

about Fairyland and all the magical creatures who live there, then the fairies will be in danger," Kirsty said. "People might try to catch them and put them in zoos or museums. . . . It would be terrible."

Isabella shivered when she heard that. Her wings trembled. "We can't let that happen," she insisted. "Thank goodness this part of the park is empty and there's no one here to see him." She turned to Flutter. "The goblin stole my magic wand. And to answer your other question, I have no idea why he's

spraying those cans. Maybe I should
ask him."

With that, the little fairy impulsively
flew from the branch and zoomed
straight toward the goblin.

## Lots of Butterflies

Kirsty and Rachel followed their fairy friend.

"Hey!" Isabella called out. She was hovering a safe distance from the goblin, her hands on her hips. "What on earth are you doing, spraying that air freshener everywhere?"

The goblin puffed out his chest. "I'm being green, of course," he said. "I'm getting rid of air pollution by making the air fresh."

Isabella stared at him. "No, you've got it all wrong," she said. "People use air freshener inside buildings — to cover up bad smells." She folded her arms across her chest. "Although, frankly, they should just open a window. That will help clean the air, not just hide the stinky smell."

The goblin looked annoyed. "*You're* the one who's got it wrong," he said. "I'm a good reader and I know what it says on these cans: Air Freshener." He pointed at each word

as he read it, and an expression of pride spread across his face.

"My plan is working very well," he bragged. "The air smells really nice now."

Isabella narrowed her eyes. "But air freshener isn't natural. It's made of hundreds of chemicals. With all your spraying, you've released those chemicals into the air. Eventually, those same chemicals will soak down into the earth. They could really hurt the soil and plants."

The goblin looked huffy. "Keep your nose out of my business," he warned. "Or I'll make *you* smell a little nicer!" Then he aimed the can right at the fairies, and ran toward them, spraying thick clouds of air freshener in their direction!

"Quick!" Rachel yelled. "Take cover!"

She and her friends dove into some nearby bushes, where the leaves would protect them from the spray.

"The chemicals in that stuff could damage our wings," Isabella said anxiously. "That goblin is a real pest!"

"Yes, he's a nuisance, isn't he?" came a
little voice from behind them. The three
fairies and Flutter turned. Flutter let out
a gasp of delight.

There was
a whole
crowd of
butterflies
in the
bushes,
all with
bright wings
and friendly
faces!

"Hello," said a butterfly with pale
yellow wings at the front of the pack.
"Nice work trying to stop that green
guy. He's been spraying those cans all

day—that's why we're hiding in here."
She wiggled her antennae at Flutter.
"Haven't seen you around here before.
My name's Goldie. And this
is Shimmer, Flit,
Willow . . ."
  Flutter was
delighted to
meet all the
butterflies. She
bobbed a happy
little hello to
each of them.
"I'm Flutter, and
this is Isabella,
Rachel, and Kirsty. Oh, it's wonderful to
see all of you!" she cried. "I've been so
lonely."

"It's nice to meet you, too." Flit smiled. She had striking red and blue markings. "Aren't you an unusual color? I've never seen a gray butterfly before."

Flutter's antennae drooped. "My wings look really boring next to all of yours," she said in a small voice. "I wish I was colorful, too."

A cornflower-blue butterfly put a kindly wing around Flutter. "I think your gray wings are very stylish," she said. "And we all know that it's what's

on the inside that counts."

"Yes, that's true," said Goldie. "Will you stay with us for a while, Flutter? You'd be very welcome. This park is usually a lovely place to live—although not at the moment, unfortunately. What *is* that green fellow doing?"

They peeked out to see that the goblin was still squirting air freshener up into the sky, in big fragrant clouds.

Rachel caught the smell in her

nose, and she let out a sneeze. *"Aaaaah-choo!* We've really got to stop him," she said.

"I agree!" said Kirsty. She looked thoughtful. "But how?"

# Get That Wand!

The three fairies fell silent, each trying to
think up a plan of action. As she racked
her brain for a good idea, Kirsty noticed
that the goblin had become quiet, too.
She peeked out and saw that he was
shaking his air-freshener cans, then
scowling and throwing them on the
ground. "They're empty," she realized
out loud. "He ran out of the spray!"

The friends watched as the goblin tried the cans one by one, but there wasn't anything left in them. The goblin wasn't happy and kicked at the empty cans. Then he took the wand from his belt and tried waving it over the pile. "Magic yourselves full again!" he commanded— but nothing happened.

"This is our chance," Rachel whispered to Kirsty and Isabella. "He can't threaten us with the air freshener if it's all gone. Maybe we can snatch Isabella's wand before he figures out how to use it!"

"I agree," said Isabella. "Come on, we'll try to surprise him."

The fairies zoomed out of the bushes toward the goblin. A look of panic fell over his face, and he pointed the wand at them. "Freeze!" he commanded, but once again, nothing happened. He shook the wand irritably. "Always works when Jack Frost says it," he grumbled to himself. "Work, you silly wand! Freeze those fairies!"

Isabella raised an eyebrow. "What *he* doesn't know is that a fairy's wand can never be used to do harm," she whispered to Kirsty and Rachel. "So don't worry. He won't be able to cast any freezing magic over us—or any other horrible spells, either!" She grinned. "Let's try and grab it."

"If Kirsty and I fly around his head, maybe he'll be distracted, and you can take the wand, Isabella," Rachel suggested.

"That's good thinking," Kirsty said. "Let's try it!"

Kirsty and Rachel began zooming around the goblin, both in different directions. He went cross-eyed, trying to keep up with them. "Can't catch me!" Rachel giggled as she whooshed over one of his big green ears.

The goblin swiped at the girls, trying to bat them away with his big hands.

"Get away!" he yelled, sounding grumpy. "You just watch it or . . . or . . ." He scratched his head, trying to think of a threat.

"Or I'll tickle you with this wand!" He waved it in midair. "Yeah — that's what I'll do. Goblins are very ticklish — I bet fairies are as well."

He began jabbing the wand at them, as if he were a swordfighter, trying to tickle them with the end of it.

Then, as he waved the wand around, Isabella suddenly caught hold of its other end. She held on with all her might. "Help me," she called to Kirsty and Rachel. "We can pull it out of his grasp!"

Rachel and

Kirsty flew to help their friend at once,
and all three of them pulled at the wand,
trying to tug it from the goblin's hand.
Unfortunately, the goblin was much
stronger. He flicked the wand
with force — and flung
all three fairies off the
end of it. They
tumbled down
toward the
bushes.

"Help!" cried Rachel as she plunged
backward.

Flutter flew out with some of her new butterfly friends. "Are you OK?" she asked, as the three fairies crashed into the leaves.

Kirsty wriggled free. "I'm fine," she said, feeling comforted by the soft breeze from Flutter's wingbeats. It actually tickled a bit, she thought . . . And then it struck her. Hadn't the goblin said that *he*

was ticklish? She grinned. "I just had a great idea!" she said.

Rachel smiled back at her friend. She couldn't wait to hear Kirsty's plan. It was sure to be a great one.

# Ticklish
# Goblin

Kirsty beckoned the butterflies closer and
told them her idea. "Do you think you
could swarm around the goblin and
tickle him with the tips of your wings?"
she asked. "If we can get him to really
giggle, he won't be able to concentrate
on holding the wand . . . and hopefully
we can grab it!"

Flutter beat her wings eagerly. "Sure!"

she said. "That sounds fun. Are the rest of you up for that?"

The other butterflies looked excited, too.

"Absolutely!" said Flit. "Let's do it!"

The butterflies flew out of the hedge in a multicolored stream and swirled around the goblin, fluttering just close enough to his head and body so their wing tips brushed against his skin.

"Oohhh . . . *ooh*, that tickles," he sputtered,

hunching forward helplessly. "Hee-hee . . .
*Ooh!* Ha-ha-ha!"

Soon the goblin was breathless with
giggles. His whole body shook as he
twisted and turned, trying to get away
from the ticklish butterflies. And
then Rachel spotted
the wand slip from
his fingers and
tumble to the
ground — the
plan had
worked!

Rachel,
Kirsty, and
Isabella
immediately
swooped down toward the fallen wand.

As soon as Isabella reached out and touched the wand, it shrank down to its Fairyland size. It immediately lit up and glowed between her fingers.

"Hooray!" Isabella cheered, twirling the wand like a bandleader's baton. "We did it! Nice work, butterflies!"

"Yes, thanks, butterflies! You can stop now," Kirsty called. She, Rachel, and Isabella flew a safe distance away.

The butterflies fluttered behind them.

Now alone, the goblin collapsed onto
the ground, still giggling uncontrollably.
Then the expression on his face changed
to anger as he realized he no longer
had the wand. "Hey!" he
shouted as he saw it
in Isabella's
hand. "That's
mine!"

"Oh, no it isn't,"
Isabella retorted.
"It's mine—
and I'm
keeping it.
I think it's
time you

went home now, before anyone spots
you!"

The goblin scowled and stomped off, muttering something about not taking orders from silly fairies. Rachel gave a cheer and turned to smile at Kirsty. She noticed her friend was looking at something else. "Is that *Flutter*?" Kirsty asked, puzzled.

Rachel couldn't see the butterfly anywhere at first. She stared where Kirsty was pointing. "But that's a blue butterfly," she said, confused. "Unless . . . Flutter, is that really you? You're not gray anymore!"

Flutter glanced at her wings and gave a squeak of delight. "I'm blue, I'm blue!" she cried, flying a figure eight in excitement. "Look at my lovely wings!"

"The gray on Flutter's wings must have been dirt from the pollution in the air," Kirsty realized. "Just like the flowers we saw near the movie theater, Rachel."

"Yes, and all that tickling must have brushed off the gray dust," Rachel figured out. She smiled at the happy butterfly. "You look great, Flutter!"

Isabella flew over and gave Flutter a little kiss. "Now that I have my wand, I can start cleaning up the air in this town," she said, "so no butterflies have to have soot-covered wings again!" She smiled. "I'll start with the parks and green areas. Trees are amazing at absorbing carbon dioxide and turning it into oxygen, which we can breathe. More trees and fewer cars, that's what we need!" Her eyes fell upon the discarded spray cans that were still lying on the ground. "But first, I'm going to do a little cleaning up right here. . . ."

She waved her wand and a flood of
magical blue sparkles swirled from it and
onto the cans. Kirsty and Rachel
watched as, one by one,
the cans sailed
through the
air to the
nearest
recycling
bin, where
they
dropped
inside.

Kirsty,
Rachel, and
the butterflies
all cheered, and
Isabella made a little
curtsey.

"Thank you, girls, you were fabulous," she said, hugging them one at a time. "Now I should send you back to Seabury. It's almost time for you to meet your parents."

"Good-bye, Isabella," said Kirsty. "I hope your clean-up magic goes well."

"We'll do what we can to help, too," Rachel promised. "Bye!"

Isabella waved her wand and with a whirl of glittering fairy magic, the two girls found themselves in Seabury once  again, back to their normal sizes. They walked toward the movie theater to find their parents.

"Wow, look at that!" Kirsty said as a street car went by, heading for the seaside. "I'd love to go on one of those while we're on vacation."

"Much more fun than traveling by car," Rachel said.

"And when we're back at home, I'll ask my teacher if we can do a project about different ways to get to school, other than using the car. I should get out my old scooter."

"Or a skateboard would be fun!" Kirsty laughed.

As they approached the theater, they could see crowds of people exiting after having just seen a movie there. "That was so exciting!" Kirsty and Rachel heard a boy say to his friend.

The girls exchanged glances. "Not half

64

as exciting as our fairy adventures,
I bet!" Rachel whispered with a grin.

Kirsty smiled. "Let's hope we have
some more adventures with the Earth
Fairies very soon!" she said happily.

Rachel and Kirsty found Nicole and Isabella's missing magic wands. Now it's time for them to hel

# Edie
## the Garden Fairy!

Join their next adventure
in this special sneak peek. . . .

# Project Green

"It's another beautiful day, Kirsty!" Rachel Walker exclaimed happily as she and her best friend, Kirsty Tate, hurried along a winding country lane. The blue sky above them was dotted with fluffy white clouds, and the sun was warm on their faces. "Isn't Rainspell Island just the most *magical* place?"

"I can't think of anywhere I'd rather go on vacation," Kirsty replied, gazing across the lush green fields. The aquamarine sea sparkled in the distance and seagulls wheeled through the crisp, salty air.

The Tates and the Walkers had arrived on the island three days ago to spend the fall break there.

"It's great that we're helping to keep Rainspell clean and beautiful, isn't it, Rachel?" Kirsty added. "Do you have the flyer that came yesterday?"

Rachel pulled the fluyer out of her pocket. PROJECT GREEN was written at the top, and underneath it read:

*Would YOU like to help the Rainspell Gardening Club make a NEW garden out of an area of unused land? Then please join us at our site on Butterfly Lane tomorrow. Wear old clothes!*

"I'm glad we decided to volunteer," Kirsty said as they studied the flyer. "We might have our friends the Earth Fairies to help us with the environment, but we humans have to do our part, too!"

Rachel nodded. Rainspell Island was a very special place because it was where she and Kirsty had first become good friends with the fairies. Since then the girls had shared many magical, amazing adventures while helping the fairies outwit cold, sly Jack Frost and his goblins.

But now it was Rachel and Kirsty's turn to ask the fairies for help. When the girls had arrived on Rainspell Island, they'd been shocked to see lots of litter scattered across the golden beach. They decided to ask the king and queen of Fairyland to help clean up the human world with fairy magic. . . .

# RAINBOW magic™

# Which Magical Fairies Have You Met?

- ☐ The Rainbow Fairies
- ☐ The Weather Fairies
- ☐ The Jewel Fairies
- ☐ The Pet Fairies
- ☐ The Dance Fairies
- ☐ The Music Fairies
- ☐ The Sports Fairies
- ☐ The Party Fairies
- ☐ The Ocean Fairies
- ☐ The Night Fairies
- ☐ The Magical Animal Fairies
- ☐ The Princess Fairies
- ☐ The Superstar Fairies
- ☐ The Fashion Fairies
- ☐ The Sugar & Spice Fairies

# RAINBOW magic™

# Which Magical Fairies Have You Met?

**3 stories in each one!**

- ❏ Joy the Summer Vacation Fairy
- ❏ Holly the Christmas Fairy
- ❏ Kylie the Carnival Fairy
- ❏ Stella the Star Fairy
- ❏ Shannon the Ocean Fairy
- ❏ Trixie the Halloween Fairy
- ❏ Gabriella the Snow Kingdom Fairy
- ❏ Juliet the Valentine Fairy
- ❏ Mia the Bridesmaid Fairy
- ❏ Flora the Dress-Up Fairy
- ❏ Paige the Christmas Play Fairy
- ❏ Emma the Easter Fairy
- ❏ Cara the Camp Fairy
- ❏ Destiny the Rock Star Fairy
- ❏ Belle the Birthday Fairy
- ❏ Olympia the Games Fairy
- ❏ Selena the Sleepover Fairy
- ❏ Cheryl the Christmas Tree Fairy
- ❏ Florence the Friendship Fairy
- ❏ Lindsay the Luck Fairy
- ❏ Brianna the Tooth Fairy
- ❏ Autumn the Falling Leaves Fairy
- ❏ Keira the Movie Star Fairy
- ❏ Addison the April Fool's Day Fairy

## ■SCHOLASTIC

Find all of your favorite fairy friends at
**scholastic.com/rainbowmagic**

HIT entertainment